REAGENT PRESS
PRESENTS

ABSOLUTES &
OTHER STORIES

ROBERT STANEK
BESTSELLING AUTHOR

Absolutes & Other Stories

Reagent Press
Published by Virtual Press, Inc.

Cover design & illustration by Robert Stanek
ISBN-13: 978-1-5754-5155-8
ISBN-10: 1-57545-155-7

REAGENT PRESS
www.reagentpress.com

Reagent Press Books by Robert Stanek

Ruin Mist Chronicles
Keeper Martin's Tale, Book 1
Kingdom Alliance, Book 2
Fields of Honor, Book 3
Mark of the Dragon, Book 4

Ruin Mist Dawn of the Ages
Rulers of Right, Book 1
Knights of the Blood, Book 2
Wardens of the Word, Book 3

Ruin Mist Chronicles (Dark Path)
Elf Queen's Quest, Book 1

Ruin Mist Heroes, Legends & Beyond
Magic of Ruin Mist
Sovereign Rule

Magic Lands
Journey Beyond the Beyond
Into the Stone Land

Visit Reagent Press online
www.**reagentpress**.com

TABLE OF CONTENTS

SILENCE IS GOLDEN

SILENCE IS GOLDEN

Ev cooed in Rin's ear, pressed her body tight against his. She kissed him, full and deep. "I've really got to. I can't be late."

"Only a few moments more," said Rin, "You're going to Ehrmolihrn-7 and the shuttle doesn't leave for another hour."

Ev stood and went to the mirror, smiling as she combed her long scarlet locks. She was pleased. She performed brilliantly. "I've earned the promotion. Can't you just be happy for me?"

"What about the day off? What will I tell the kids?"

"Duty calls—the twins will understand. Besides, I'm meeting Director Finn."

"UFC Director Finn?"

Ev kissed Rin on the cheek. "This will go well," she said. "I'll present to the Director and come home. This was the last. Traitors can only hide for so long—it's all done now."

Silence is Golden

A light knock came to the door. The door swept open. "Mommy, mommy," shouted Marty and Penn. "Come look!"

Ev pulled her robe from the side of the mirror, slipping it on before wrapping her arms around the boys—her boys. "Mommy's got to get ready. Show daddy." She smiled, releasing the embrace reluctantly. She watched the boys cross to Rin, jump onto the bed.

A pillow fight ensued—it always did. She moved away from the mirror quickly, catlike as she hurried into the bathroom, hoping Rin and the boys didn't see her tears.

She closed the bathroom door, turned on the faucet, collapsing to the floor. Anguish and tears took her as never before. She lay there, trembling, crying, trying to pull herself together. She looked up, saw herself in the long mirror suddenly thinking she looked like a scared little girl. She got it together then. If there's one thing she wasn't anymore, it was a scared little girl huddling in corners as plasma bombs exploded all around her.

She rinsed her face, turned off the faucet then hurriedly penciled in her mascara, eyeliner and lipstick. Her uniform was there, pressed and waiting. She tucked her long shirt in as she went into the bedroom to find her black leather boots.

Rin and the boys were in the kitchen. She heard them singing the breakfast song—a silly song of soggy cereal that was the only thing that would get Marty and Penn to eat in the

*   *

morning. She kissed the boys, hugging them as tightly as she had before. She kissed Rin, whispering in his ear, "Take this. Play it after I've gone. You'll know what to do then."

She ran from the kitchen, into the foyer, out of the house with Rin calling after her. She knew he was confused. He wouldn't understand at first but he would know what to do. The safety of the boys depended on it.

She was pulling the hydro out of the garage when he ran out of the house. She pretended not to see him, pressing Engage and slipping into the morning sky before he could do or say anything that would change her mind. She knew in that moment, that instant between heartbeats when she saw his eyes reflected in the rearview mirror and the hydro raced away, that she would never see him or the boys again. She accepted that—had no other choice but to accept that as the alternative was something she just couldn't endure.

Fifteen minutes later, she was strapped in waiting for the shuttle to depart for Ehrmolihrn-7. She wasn't afraid anymore, she was beyond that. She reminded herself that she would smile for the director as she gave her tactics review. Then she would wait, accept what came next. She wasn't afraid of the silence anymore—silence was golden.

The shuttle launched. Tsetingaen-17 fell away behind her. She didn't look back, only ahead, but that didn't slow her thoughts or stop her mind from replaying the digix. She

*   *

wondered then as a tear well up in her eye if Marty and Penn would understand it all some day. She hoped they would but knew Rin never would.

■■■

My dearest, please forgive me. I know I promised—I did try. But one against the many could never hope to win, to have hoped at all was struggle enough. Here at the last, I remember it all and it seems a sin for which I cannot be redeemed. Indeed, I do not expect to be redeemed nor want to be redeemed.

Now that I'm faced with it, I do not expect you to understand. I'll take with my own hands the one thing you should have taken. For you, you should not find redemption either. Your sin is greater than mine and you should never again find that which you seek but that doesn't mean shouldn't know truth—the real and simple truth that you'll find once this thing between us is no more.

To find truth, you must look to the past—2197—and the real beginning: the treaty signing on Ehrmolihrn-7. Then there had been fourteen million forms of Majority verbal communications, commonly called glots or languages.

The UFC had had the need to represent them all, and hence the dawning of the age of the Polyglot and the Poly-li-tech. Who could have known that two centuries later the respected and once vaulted title of Poly-li-technician would become the basis for high treason to the Majority?

*   *

The First Crusade, as it was called, began in 2394. History records show that ancient wars had been fought for politics, ethnic differences, and religion. The Majority fancied themselves Purists, though they did not strive to eradicate racial or political differences, or even to abolish religious practices which had been outlawed since 2315.

Their goal was to purify the universe and bond it by one Majority language. Their faction was over three trillion strong then, and they arrogantly seized control of the UFC, reprogramming its lawkeeper system to do their bidding.

The First Crusade ended in 2679 when Majority-1 declared the universe pure. But we the last linguists survived, ironically sanctioned away by the same faction that wished our demise—Majority-1 wanted to be ready and vigilant should speech diversity return.

By 2695, we were little more than house slaves, forced to scribe out our Minority languages. According to Majority-1, no language could proliferate with only one native speaker and so exactly thirteen million nine hundred ninety-nine thousand nine hundred ninety-nine of us labored in Record Hall on Gyandress-4. We were then categorized as Silenced, later officially titled Moribund as one by one after transcription, we as heretics to the UFC and Majority-1 were given our final sentencing.

In 2745, lead by the heretic Duilaird, the Second Minority

Silence is Golden

Front was established and the Second Crusade began. The First Crusade had lasted over three centuries, the Second had just dawned. Majority-1 decided the title Moribund was incitant and had caused the outbreak. All defunct glots were thus officially recategorized as Silenced. But by then, it was too late.

I speak now in this the year 31 M-1, thirty-one years after Majority-1 declared Final Universal Purity. It is a testament to the last linguist, spoken for all those that will someday follow in my footsteps, or so I hope—and at the very least, for you.

Even as I write this, I know they come for me—I know who it is that betrayed me. I do not fear or regret; I've given in so deeply to both that I am beyond them. I accept my guilt as well. I am guilty of high treason three times over: guilty on the account that I am Poly-li-tech, guilty that I proliferate diversity, guilty that I am a recorder of culture and history. Once fourteen million languages and millions of proud peoples existed, now there is only Majority-1.

Duilaird liberated us in 2745 and while our numbers were in the mere millions, we spread through the galaxy like a diverse storm. It took only one speaker to rekindle a lust for lost heritage.

Duilaird directed us to return to our home worlds and spread our known tongues to any and all who would listen. Within two decades we became billions and years later

*   *

trillions. In the end, it took a thousand years to stop what a single, raised voice had started.

I retain hope that there are others out there somewhere in the endless spans of the universe, others who possess the skill to speak with diversity, others who can proliferate speech diversity. Yet, as far as I know, at my passing the last disparate glot will be forever silenced.

My heart is skipping, my voice shaking, hands trembling. It will be only a matter of hours now. I cannot run: there is no where left to run to. I cannot hide: there is nowhere they cannot find me.

I will not let them take anything else, nor let you take your prize. I'll fall to my own silence and bring about eternity in my own way. And thus, it is my hope that they will not win, that you will not find redemption.

My hope against hope is that some small pocket somewhere remains and will fight back against Majority-1. Maybe they will succeed where we have failed.

I speak aloud to an empty room in a tongue that is proclaimed silenced, I am proud. Oft I've wondered what Duilaird would have thought of such an end. Would he have thought it glorious? Or would he be as deeply saddened by it as am I?

Years ago I relished the fading and growing of the echoes, though I do not now. They come ever closer, tracking the deceitful echoes of my words, my words in a traitor's tongue.

I wonder if the hunters know they will be the hunted once diversity is stamped out. For in the end, no one must know that any voice other than Majority-1 existed. What will you think then dearest? Will it be you who takes even when you know what must come next?

You've led well. I commend you. I knew your training would serve you, but do you really know who it is that you serve? Will you find redemption in this life or the next—I think not.

My heart grows heavy; the end is here. The silence comes. I say now a final prayer and express my eternal thanks to Duilaird the Heretic. Had I to do it all again, I'd have begged to go first—begged as I'm sure Marten begged—but I would have taken you with me. I wouldn't have had regret either.

The silence comes. I welcome it—your silence comes as well.

■■■

The shuttle docking roused Ev to conscious thoughts. She stepped with purpose, not surprised to see an escort board the shuttle and approach. Another time, the escort would have been considered an honor contingent. Today though she knew that if she elected otherwise, the escort would follow anyway becoming more guard then escort.

She smiled graciously, nodding to Malleck, the Officer of

*   *

the Watch. "Another long day?"

"Another long day." Malleck hid a grin. "Are you to the Director?"

Ev nodded. Nothing on Ehrmolihrn-7 had changed. She walked the long hall from the shuttle, her eyes seeing the long line of gray uniforms on either side of the walkway but her mind only on what was ahead. "I need to make a stop first. It'll only be a moment."

Malleck grabbed Ev's elbow as she turned to a side hall. "Orders: no stops. We're to go straight to Central."

"And you're to hold my hand while I tinkle?"

Malleck released his grip. He called to one of the female escorts.

"So formal today?"

"Orders."

Ev shrugged, hurried down the side hall. The female escort followed. The woman's lavatory was at the end of the hall. She paused briefly outside the door, casually looking back, judging the distance between her and Mellack. It was at least 50 meters.

She walked the length of the bathroom, going to the last stand. She squatted to the toilet as the escort looked on. "Any chance for privacy? Some things just weren't meant to be done with an audience."

The escort glared.

Ev waited until she heard movement that wasn't hers or the escorts. She waited for the movement to go away, for the door to open and close. She waited a bit more to be sure no one else was in the room.

The escort cleared her throat. "Time."

"What are you serious? I can't control how long it takes—it takes as long as it takes."

"Orders. Let's go."

Ev stood, straightened her uniform, marched from the bathroom. Mellack was waiting, nodding approval at the female escort as she took her place with the others.

Central was thirty minutes away by hydro. The Director's offices a few minutes after that. Ev was silent the entire way.

Director Fynn greeted her. The double doors closed behind her. The adjacent meeting room was empty as was the secretary's position at the front desk.

Director Fynn stretched out his arm, pointing the way to the meeting room. "I trust it was a success?"

"Very much so," said Ev. "We've been able to confirm it as well." Ev went to the review board then, walking Director Finn through each moment of the operation. "Everything according to plan. No surprises."

"I didn't expect there to be with your planning. You really are the best."

Caught up in the moment, Ev's eyes lit up and she smiled.

*   *

"Tactics are what I live for."

"Indeed." Director Finn went to the review board. "This room. Can you tell me again what happened after you broke through the plasma shielding?"

"UFC 707.B4A."

"By the book?"

"I made sure. I carried it out myself."

The director looked up, straight into Ev's eyes. "You didn't have any problems?"

"Is this leading somewhere?"

Director Finn thumped the digix in his hand. "Did you view or make copies?"

"Eyes only. Procedure." Ev said it coolly but inside her stomach twisted in knots.

Director Finn opened his palm, tapped the tiny display screen. The digix holograph filled the space between him and Ev. "Do you recognize this face?"

"UFC 707.B4A: the silencing."

"He's the one and you're sure?" Ev nodded. "And you're the one he's speaking to aren't you?"

The weight of the universe crushed Ev into a seat. She'd been waiting for this moment, preparing for it, but dreading it all the same. "I am."

"Then you know the truth of it?" Director Finn said it as coolly as Ev had spoken previously.

Silence is Golden

"I do." Ev looked away, down the long mahogany table, thinking it ironic just then that the table was the only non-artificial thing in the room. "And you do as well."

Director Finn stood at the back of Ev's chair, putting his hands on her shoulders. His touch gentle at first became firm, then forceful as he spoke, "According to UFC 707.B4A, I pass silencing on you. Don't struggle, it'll be over soon."

Ev didn't struggle. In her mind's eye, she saw and heard the twins. They were running, playing. Their voices echoing down the halls. She knew also that in a matter of moments the escorts would come through the doors. Mellack would phaser the director, destroy the digix, then turn the phaser on the other escorts.

The surprise in waiting was a second cleanup crew, the one that would take out Mellack. Ev had seen them—her trip to the lavatory hadn't been about tinkling.

Behind the cleanup crew would come others and by day's end, there would be no more Central. But it wouldn't stop there, the UFC programming would continue. If someone was doing the cleaning, someone was giving the orders: someone always knows so the edict that no one can know must loop and that loop would sooner or later carry the edict back to Majority-1. Ev was only sorry that she would miss that moment, that moment when Majority-1 realized they had become the hunted and that their end was near.

AUGUST RAINS

AUGUST RAINS

The halls lined with well-worn steel lockers stood silent; no more laughter, no more children, ever. Principal John Anderson—Mr. Anderson to his students, John to his colleagues, Johnny to precious Angelica who left seven summers ago—strolled down the long empty hall one last time.

"Forty-two years," he whispered to the fading echoes of his footsteps, and to Angelica.

He caught a glimpse of Autumn leaves through well-frosted windows. The leaves, brown, gold and red from the two great maples that guarded the entrance, littered the central walkway; the walkway that ran straight and true to the Jane's School Elementary flagpole. Beyond the flagpole,

August Rains

School Circle met East and 3rd. Beyond that lay things John didn't want to think about.

A northerly wind began to gust and John whispered after it, "Old man winter isn't your time."

By now he had reached the opposite end of the long dividing hall. His brief stroll was at an end. He turned to look back. K through three were lined up on his left; four through six, his right. At the far end, waited his nearly deserted office. At the near end, the music room, less piano, students and teacher. The piano, purchased in '57, had served thirty consecutive years. It had been there for the school band, summer singing lessons, little Bobby Ferillo who had earned a fellowship, and even the church choir auxiliary after the fire of '72.

Memories of music and a soft, raised voice carried his eyes to the empty playground. The merry-go-round was turning in the sharp wind and every now and again he could hear its shrill squeak. "Beverlie Smithe bought it for $15.00 at the auction, Angelica. I nearly wept, yet I just couldn't let myself buy it. Really though, I had no place to put it... I remember the first time I heard your voice; it was the first time we met: September 5th, 1957. As if it were yesterday, I remember. Teaching English to the fourth grade class right next door, I was. The singing and playing, soft at first, raised me to a start because there hadn't been a piano the previous year, and of course there hadn't been a music teacher the previous year either.

"The voice was sweet don't get me wrong but I was trying to teach a class of unruly nine and ten year olds English and it just couldn't be done with music and singing drowning me out. Oh yes, I'm sure you remember. How could you forget?"

Leaves, brown, gold and red, were chasing round the merry-go-round in a great flurry—up, up, up, carried on a stout tuft, then left to swirl lazily down and finally settle around the still moaning merry-go-round. The first rain drops spattered the glass of the padlocked red doors as John looked on.

"In '57 didn't need padlocks or chains," muttered John as the PA tweaked and then hissed.

"Mr. An-der-son?" called out an unsure voice, "Mr. Anderson? I gotta lock up now."

John crooned, "Few more minutes!" Then turned back to rain spattering the now muddied glass and wind kicking up Autumn leaves.

"Remember little Tommy Ferillo, Bobby's brother? You always said he'd never amount to much and never cast a shadow in his brother's footsteps. Well, he didn't, but there he is turning me to the street just the same... Our visits keep growing shorter and shorter, don't they?"

John turned back to face K through three on his left and four through six on his right. The street beyond the flagpole

*   *

seemed suddenly close. He took the first and most important step back down the long, empty hall lined with worn metal lockers. Again he listened to the echoes of his footsteps—step, drag, step drag, old age. He'd sworn he'd never use a cane and he hadn't, even when Autumn rains made his rheumatoid arthritis flare and walking became God's only chore.

He stopped at the door to the fourth grade. The door's glass, covered in the dust of years, was dark and solemn. John twisted the knob. The door was locked. But never mind that old lock had never worked even on the day it had been installed by Henry Green the town's one and only locksmith forty odd years ago. Jimmying the lock required only a few sharp twists. 1,2,3, click!

"The desks are all gone. Over to the new school I'd reckon. But never you mind, I won't be going there. 'Retirement,' they said. I said, 'You'd have to close the school first.' Well, you know they did. I never expected it. Never did. 'Progress,' they called it. Well, if that is progress, I don't want any part of it."

Footsteps outside the door broke the reverie. John turned. "Mr. Anderson, you in there? I gotta close up now. Cindy and the kids are waiting for me to take them to the new Mc Donald's, just opened you know. If it's jam packed with gawkers and lunch crowd by the time we get there, I'll never hear the end of it. And that storm's really coming in off the lake!"

*   *

"How's Bob, Tom, you see him much these days?"

"The Nam took 'im in '71, Mr. Anderson. Are you all right? You don't look well. Your face is much paler than it was this morning." John took a step toward the door, then dragged his right foot. "Mr. Anderson, did you hear what I said, that storm's..."

"I can feel it clear to my bones, going to be a mighty powerful storm. Better tell Cindy and the kids that Mac Donald's can wait."

John pushed away the extended hand, took another step. "Come back every Autumn don't you, Mr. Anderson?" asked Tom.

"Got to see if they tore her down, just got to know. Then I can endure winter snow, spring flowers, and summer sun—all the things she loved so." John stopped, turned on his left heel. Tom jumped to support his right side as he teetered. "See there, the fifth grade. Only six desks there in '51. One more the next year, two less the year after."

The two turned, ambled down the entry corridor; Tom continuing to lurk at John's right waiting to catch the other if he fell. Shadows from the two great oaks, their leaves mostly fallen revealing bare boughs extending to the darkened heavens, lay about the entryway. Between the trunks, John glimpsed School Circle, the flagpole and the street beyond.

Chased on by strong gusts, rain fell in a thick and ceaseless torrent. Wet leaves pressed against the glass of the entryway. A flash of lightning and a rumbling clap of thunder made dark skies seem much more ominous. The lights flickered twice, then the sound of wind-chased raindrops returned.

"Wait, I have an umbrella around here someplace—Cindy made me take it with this morning," said Tom, "Say would you like to come over for lunch? She'll be less sore, the kids less disappointed, if I bring over a guest. They were sure looking forward to Mc Donald's. They've been watching those commercials on TV. You know the ones for the Big Mac. Ever had one?"

"Don't have a TV, never had the need. Never had a Big Mac either."

Tom turned back around. "Hey what'd you know, I found it. You'll be coming over then, yes?" Tom opened the door and unfolded the umbrella. The outside air was full of dampness and chill.

"Tell Cindy and the kids: Hello. I got a long drive around the lake ahead. She loved to drive in rain storms. I never quite understood why."

Tom folded the umbrella and stepped back inside. "She, your wife you mean? It was terrible. They finally cut down that oak tree on the corner of Main and Center when it took Mr. Miller and his wife during the blizzard last year. Did you know, we, mom, Cindy and I, visited the hospital in July on her

*   *

birthday. She still dotes on what you and her did for Bob. She always says if the Nam wouldn't of took him, he'd have been a world-class pianist... World-class... The rains not going to stop you know."

"I know. I just needed a bit of a rest is all. Will you walk me to my car?"

"I can't twist your arm to come over?"

"No, I'll be all right. You just walk me to my car. I have a long drive around the lake ahead. I like to listen to the rain slap at the windshield. It helps me forget. But you can bet I'll be back next autumn and I might just take that offer if it still stands."

"You can count on it, Mr. Anderson. You're always welcome, always..."

ABSOLUTES

CHAPTER ONE: CRYOTERRAFORM

The light pulsated, its amber glow intermittently bathing the lab. The hum of the elevator as it descended, a faint whir growing closer, had everyone's attention. I kissed Kendyll on the cheek and whispered in her ear, "It's been a wonderful 17 years. If we follow the plan, we can make it through this. Trust me."

She burst into tears and ran from the lab. I watched her go, my legs going numb as I sought to chase after her. I glanced at my watch as the elevator came within sight. It was 23:45. Fifteen minutes to midnight. Fifteen minutes until doom, January 15, 2365.

Absolutes

The team had worked through the night for days. We were one step away from everlasting breakthrough and now Project IV decided to send out their goons and the brilliant goon who was going to save the day. One of my colleagues kidded me once that what we were doing was akin to exposing lime Jello to the vacuum of space, supercooling it, then condensing it in order to figure out why it's the color green it is.

I hoped goons liked lime Jello.

The elevator stopped. Everything stopped. I swung my eyes around the lab, from the monitor that showed security waiting on the surface to the elevator doors as they slowly opened. I could hear the pulleys winding, the levers moving, the doors slowly retracting.

I waited, my heart pounding in my ears, my eyes leveled on the spot where I imagined the face of the brilliant goon — Project IV's hope — should be, but instead of seeing a face, I saw a mop of rusty brown hair.

As I panned down, I saw blue eyes and a galaxy of freckles. Still lower, a T-shirt that proudly announced "I found It," then genuine Bermuda shorts as florescent a green as the green in lime Jello, and finally a pair of dirty yellow sneakers.

I found myself gritting my teeth as I stepped forward, hand extended. Eighty-two days into this latest attempt, I was confronted with a kid from Moonbase III. Worse still, I knew his name, would never forget that name: Krzysztof Steelbridge.

*   *

Eighteen hours into the current workday, I suddenly found the humor of the Jello statement. Yet I wasn't laughing, I was near tears. I didn't need this kid anymore. We were on the verge of our own breakthrough and his arrival was just an untimely interruption. I needed him two months ago, not now.

My hand jolted back to my side, I don't know what came over me, but suddenly I felt bold. I screamed, "Get off the pad you idiot!"

"That's pronounced Krzysz-tof," he said. "But you can call me Krys, everyone else does. Wow, some ride, I tell you!"

My jaw dropped. I remembered him as wet behind the ears from my classes and loud as a choir rat. "The journey's going to end real quick if you don't get off that pad," I found myself saying.

He upturned apprehensive blue eyes. "Why?"

"Stormrise," I said. "Where's your protective gear?"

"Stormrise? You need to shut everything down."

Genius? I smiled now, having stumped genius boy. The pain receded from my gut as I tossed him a protective suit. Kendyll came back into the central dome of the lab from the living cubicles. The mascara around her eyes was newly penciled in. The pale rose lipstick gone. Her beautiful high-boned cheeks were now dry.

For a moment, I caught her eye. She smiled seeing what I knew was renewed confidence mirrored in my eyes. I glanced to the monitors that showed there were more arrivals on the surface, then to my watch.

Midnight.

Kendyll began directing the efforts of the team. I turned my attention back to the common array and made sure everything was exactly focused on the single dwindling mass in the cryo-chamber's heart. A minor resonance problem captured my attention for a time, but soon I noticed the press of Krys standing behind me.

Krys tapped me on the shoulder. I turned.

"What are you doing?" he demanded, the tone of his voice pointed, as if to say he was in control. "You have to shut everything down!"

Cryoterraform. How the hell was I supposed to explain all this to some punk kid and not ruin my day? I said, hoping to say nothing that would interest him, "The array is quite simple. Focus a thin stream of photons with a micro-precise amount of energy that reacts with the center mass of atoms. The focused stream of photons bombards the larger atoms, like meteorites striking the face of old-Earth with the precise purpose of ending its rotation and bringing it to a dead stop. The slower, the colder, until the atoms are on the verge of the absolute: standing still. Others may have reached it, but no one knows its full potential—"

I bit my tongue to stop my lips from moving and wished for

*   *

a bowl of lime Jello to fill my mouth before I said something that I knew I'd regret.

Krys stared up at me. The glazed-over look in his eyes, I hoped was a good sign. Then he said. "Is cesium still the atom of choice because of the way it reacts to light?"

I laughed. Yes, cesium possessed a whole integer spin, but cesium was the atom of choice no more. "Its mass is simply too large."

"What about hydrogen? It has a whole integer spin, a boson, right?"

Yes, hydrogen was small, the smallest, and it was capable of clumping together in unlimited numbers. But its mass was simply too small. I said proudly, "Too small."

A moment later I found myself filling the silence with, "How old are you anyway, kid?"

He glared at me as if I was speaking a foreign language.

"It's English, kid… And don't answer, I don't want to know any more. My colleagues hit an invisible wall with cesium and hydrogen: They couldn't get the atoms cold enough or dense enough to form one of the most spectacular states of matter: Bose-Einstein condensation. The point where matter condenses into a single entity. An entity few have seen and no one truly understands. Cryoterraform, kid. No one has ever seen; no one has ever done it. And it all starts with an entity perhaps akin to the incredibly dense white dwarf — and that's what I am after, a miniature white dwarf, a manmade white dwarf, a miniature and super-dense, bright white star of my own design and then—"

I bit my tongue again. I'd reached the absolute, but it was the final absolute I was after. I was sure this kid who'd been here all of five minutes would get credit for it somehow. I knew it, I just knew it.

Krys smiled. I shrank back.

He said, "I can see now why the community labeled you mad, but also why your team never had a lack of financial backers—"

"Yes, Project IV was always there but only because while the other guys were at a virtual standstill, I defied the laws of nature and won for the very reason quantum mechanics confounds conventional thinkers. Label me mad if you will, but at precisely 00:15, we'll have finally reached critical density." With or without genius boy.

Call me Krys, call me Krys, label me stupid. How was I supposed to explain a lifetime to genius boy in fifteen minutes?

I turned to the technicians and Kendyll. "Stormrise in ten minutes. I've got to revert power from the field, I need it for boosting."

"Boosting?" Krys asked. "You're not supposed to—"

"Yes, boosting," I cut in. "Fasten the zippers on the suit, kid.

*   *

Where'd you get your degree from?" A diversion. I knew the answer already; he'd been in five of my classes.

"I got my—"

"No, talk while you zip."

"I did my post-doctorate work on Moonbase III. I found Top-Omega."

"How old are you, kid?"

"Twenty-three."

I knew I didn't want to know. "Well son, I'm fifty-seven, don't forget it," I spoke fast, "I don't care if you found Top-Omega or Charm-Delta. Grab those goggles there, you're going to need them eventually."

He pointed to a pair of goggles hanging from a support next to a line of protective suits. "This?"

"Yes. Do you see any other?"

"No."

"Put them on. Come back over here. Yes, over here…" I paused, and then asked, "What do you think? They said it'd never work, but there it is, developing before your very eyes with the cameras to record it. At Stormrise, I'll have reached the final absolute: the cessation of motion born out of the coldest cold — 460 degrees below zero Fahrenheit — and soon afterward, the birth of our very own super dense—"

"What's causing that vibration there?"

"What vibration, kid—" My eyes went wide. I shouted.

"Kendyll, get over here! Kendyll, where are you?

She appeared at my side.

"Switch the exterior image recorder on now and boost the levels."

She did. I watched the instrument panel, my eyes darting to the cryo-chamber.

I said, "There, that's it… Yes, that's it."

Krys exclaimed, "It's still shrinking and the glow is spectacular."

As I turned to look at him, I lost track of Kendyll. "What's happening? Kid, where'd Kendyll go?"

Krys said, "The vibration resonance is drowning out everything else, but it looks to me like she's busy with the technicians."

"Save the commentary, kid. Adjust those levels: point zero zero zero one. Kendyll?" I'm going to kill her; I'm going to kill her. Where is she? I need her.

"Point zero zero one."

"Give me that, point zero zero zero one." I turned and shouted, "Kendyll?"

Krys said, "I would've gotten it you know. Yes, I am twenty-three, but I've—"

"Save the commentary, kid. Here, keep adjusting the levels down, point zero zero zero one every fifteen seconds." The vibrations intensified, shifted. "Cryoterraform, we're almost there. Can you believe it?"

I craned my neck and peered around the lab, but couldn't see clear to the other side of the chamber. "Where's Kendyll, where's Kendyll?"

"Here, I'm here," she said, "you stubborn, old goat. You don't need to carry on so. They were having problems maintaining reversion. I've got most of the team on it. The others are — I can't hear anything over that noise. Where's it coming from?"

I pointed.

Her eyes went wide. "No?"

"Yes." I smiled.

Her eyes became great saucers. "It isn't?"

The particle cloud was completely gone now, replaced by a phenomenal glowing point of light of microscopic proportions: the source of the teeth-rattling vibrations. "It is."

She said, "It's never done that before. What's causing it?"

"I don't know. Get Gwen and Tabbith on it pronto."

The kid said, "It's feedback, feedback from the reversion processing. It's got to be."

"Who's the kid?"

I smiled at her casual nonchalance. "Dr. Margaret Kendyll, Krzysztof Steelbridge."

Kendyll stuck out her hand.

"Shake her hand, kid. She's my wife and colleague. She

won't bite." I turned back to Kendyll. "He's what Project IV sent, can you believe it? Just arrived a few minutes ago."

"You said tomorrow and the report said — Well, I was expecting—"

I shrugged. "So was I, so was I. Let's get back to work."

She said, "Don't you think the rest of the team should see this? I mean, isn't this—"

"They can gawk later. For now, I don't want them to move. Do you know how long I've waited for this? We're almost there and I don't want anything to spoil this."

"You know I do, you old fart."

I glanced at my watch. 00:13. "Stormrise in two minutes!"

Kendyll said, "I'll get Gwen and Tabbith. We'll start the survey."

Kendyll hurried away, I watched her go. To Krys I said, "Kid, you adjusting those levels?"

"Krys, and yes, I am."

"Good," I said, standing back. The nacreous point had just trebled in size.

"She's a good-looking woman," Krys said glancing over his shoulder.

"Save the commentary, kid, she's wearing a shielding suit, and she's twice your age. You still down adjusting those levels?"

Krys nodded.

*   *

"Good, worry about them and nothing else."

My heart was beating so fast, I had to sit. I backed against a cushioned lab chair and fell into it.

Krys looked down at me. "You know why Project IV sent me, don't you, doctor?"

"I don't give a good goddamn, kid... Okay now, keep that adjustment. Would you look at that?"

CHAPTER TWO: STORMRISE

One of the technicians shouted, "We've got Stormrise!"

I jumped out of the chair.

Krys said, "They sent me to replace you, doctor. Your wife would stay on of course, but you'd go back to Moonbase III."

"Save the commentary, kid, I'm not listening." I double-checked the laser array and the strength of the magnetic field inside the chamber. "What's the readout, second column, third row?"

"1 E to the minus 7. You know it doesn't matter, don't you? Even if you reach Bose-Einstein condensation, it won't matter now. They're going to replace you anyway."

Absolutes

"Kid, I reached Bose a very long time ago. That's not what I'm after."

"You reached Bose and didn't tell anyone? Who do you think you are? No wonder I'm replacing you."

"Shut up, kid, matter cessation was just the stepping off point. There's something beyond and that's what we're after."

"There is nothing beyond matter cessation, that's the ultimate state of matter. What is there beyond a standstill?" His eyes widened to unbelievably large circular globes. "What does it look like, doctor? What does Bose-Einstein condensation look like?... Good god, I've got to tell Project IV. Do you know what this means? Do you know what they'll do to you for withholding this? You'll never get a research grant ever again. You're finished, finished. You are mad, aren't you?" He paused to catch his breath.

I saw the curiosity in his eyes.

He said, "What are you looking for?"

"Absolutes. Don't you see? Einstein and Bose made the initial predictions and somewhere along the way we forgot the absolutes because we truly believed they couldn't be attained. One microkelvin and 100 atmospheres simply wasn't enough. That's what I told them."

"At condensation the natural laws don't even apply. It's something we don't understand; something half the world will never understand: A state of matter that isn't gaseous, liquid or

*   *

solid. So they send me a kid whose specialty is heating things up to solve it all. Well, there you go, kid, one supercooled, fuzzy atom. Isn't that what you wanted?"

Krys said, "Where are you going?"

"You said you're my replacement, you got the show. See you later, kid. I've got everything I need right here." I tapped my forehead. "And it's all going to stay locked up there forever."

I walked away, five or six steps, stopped.

Krys's eyes were as wide as Kendyll's beautiful performance minutes earlier. "You said there was something beyond matter cessation and that you wanted to see it. Where are you going?"

"It didn't work, kid, look at the displays. It stopped at condensation; it didn't complete the transition. One supercooled, fuzzy atom is all I ever get. The light show and noise was just an added bonus."

"But isn't that what you set out to find? Don't you see the breakthrough here?"

"Kid, I saw that four years ago. I'm tired. I'm going to bed unless of course you'd like my room too since you're replacing me." I turned to look at Kendyll. She was pretending not to notice my moment of self-tortured pity.

I shouted, "Turn it down, switch it all down!"

The lab slowly fell to silence. I heard the shuffling of feet and quiet whispers. I heard my heart pounding in my ears because my career was seconds away from re-birth or death.

"I need sleep," I muttered for the kid's sake, "sleep's the cure for all that ails you."

I walked out of Krys's eyesight and waited. My heart stopped when I heard the whine of pulleys begin to move the elevator.

Six miles to the surface. Six miles back down.

I turned my full attention to Krys.

Kendyll put her hand on his shoulder and said, "He didn't mean to yell at you, Krys. He gets like this sometimes. He'll get over it and in four hours or so he'll be inspired again."

"He said he reached Bose-Einstein condensation four years ago. That was in the first six months of the experiment. If he told Project IV, I wouldn't be here."

"He's a stubborn, old goat, Krys. He didn't want to achieve what others had achieved but couldn't reproduce. He wanted to reproduce it consistently and go beyond."

Kendyll took a deep breath. "I really thought we finally went past that stopping point. The resonance, it must've been an anomaly. I really thought that was it and so did he. I could see it in his eyes." Kendyll gasped. "Could I see it in his eyes!"

Krys said, "He said no one else knew he reached it. How long have you known?"

"I've known since day one, we all have. He's what keeps us going. He really believes there's something else."

*   *

"You mean to say that you've been going at this for nearly five years when you knew the madman had already achieved Bose-Einstein condensation? Are you as mad as he? You know I'm here to replace him, don't you? Project IV wants him back at Moonbase III so they can keep an eye on him."

"Now there's a laugh and a half. He's not mad Krys. We all knew. We all believed. I believe, Krys. If he told me the sun was blue and the sky yellow, good God, I'd believe him. Don't you understand? If you let Project IV take away his life, they'll never find another like him. No one can duplicate his findings. He really does keep all his notes in his head. Photographic memory, been that way since the day he was born fifty-seven years ago. The experiment will go with him and it will die with him."

Krys's face turned candy apple red. "You'd let him do that? I mean, you'd just let him flush it all down the drain."

"Funny thing about drains, Krys, you ever watch one? Here they rotate clockwise, where I lived on old-Earth, they rotated counterclockwise. Funny thing that. You're the one holding the plug on the drain, Krys. How old are you anyway?"

Krys frowned and said, "Twenty-three."

"Twenty-three. My youngest is twenty-four. She's doing her graduate studies. What'd you do to get here anyway?... No, don't tell me. Private tutors until you were twelve, completed your bachelor's studies at fourteen, did your graduate work at

MPI with an immediate follow on for your doctorate program. Screamed through your doctorate program and here you are, a genius at twenty-one."

"Twenty-three, and I completed the formulations on the last link of the sub-atomic puzzle. You don't recognize the name, Krzysztof Steelbridge, King Supercollider... "

Kendyll laughed. I laughed with her from the shadows.

"I don't give a damn, Krys, wrong end of the spectrum. We don't heat things up here, if you haven't noticed. You didn't invent sub-atomic particles, Krys. They always existed."

Kendyll put a hand on Krys's shoulder and stared him directly in the eye. "Have them build you another supercollider and you go back to slamming your atoms together. Leave us alone, we don't need you. Don't you see? This didn't exist until he created it. That's why we believe in him, Krys. He makes us believe. But I don't think you understand that do you?"

"No, I don't," Krys admitted.

Kendyll turned away. The laser array was silent. The machines, all silent. It seemed I could hear the heartbeats of everyone in the lab as we all listened. Then she turned back and said, "I wasn't describing you, Krys, I was describing him: Dr. Martin Schwenne. You're practically following in his footsteps and you don't even know it. You could be brilliant, a true genius with the right mentor."

She had tears in her eyes. I could tell by the quiver in her voice. "I was your age when I met him, divorced with two small children, going to college three nights a week and barely getting by. One day, I heard him speak. He was giving a lecture — I chanced into the wrong room at the wrong time, and there he was and there I was. Look at me today, I wouldn't be here if it wasn't for him."

I sucked at the air as she turned. Now I saw her clearly staring into his eyes.

"Everything's about absolutes, Krys. Either you believe or you don't. He says he'll find it. Do you believe?" She continued. "Because if you do, all you have to do is tell him and he'll go back to work. He doesn't give a damn about Project IV. Project IV doesn't give a damn about him. They pay the bills. We use the funds to keep Cryoterraform alive."

She walked him over to the array. "The atoms in the air you're breathing are zooming around at more than one thousand feet per second. Zooming, zooming, zooming. At absolute zero, atoms stand perfectly still but there's something beyond. He wants the absolute: the full transition, the new state of matter. We'll use the array to achieve a thing no one beyond these walls has every dreamed: Cryoterraform — the transformation of matter."

Krys watched Kendyll as she moved about the room.

"Can you imagine the point where matter stands absolutely still, Krys, and that which is just beyond? The point where matter isn't — a form no human has ever seen before. What happens to matter when you supercool it to 460 degrees below zero Fahrenheit and having hit the final absolute is standing absolutely still and then go just a bit further? What would it look like? Would it shine with the brightness of a hundred tiny suns? Would it be akin to a tiny and super-dense white dwarf?"

Krys tried to answer but Kendyll wouldn't let him. "Could you even imagine a tiny point of light radiating like a hundred tiny suns? Would this new form have spontaneity and change from instant to instant before our very eyes? Would it keep condensing, changing, growing? That's what Cryoterraform is, Krys, that's what it's all about. He believes, I believe—we all believe."

She pointed to the technicians in the lab. "There's something there, just beyond that stepping off point. You have to believe, Krys. It's something wonderful, something no one has ever imagined, and now you have the opportunity to be a part of that discovery or destroy a life's work. You're either on the team or off, now which is it?"

Krys was silent for a long time and just when I thought he wasn't going to say anything, he said, "God, Doctor Kendyll, I really wish I could tell you... But—"

She put a finger to his lips. "Stop there, before you say something you'll regret for the rest of your natural life, Krys.

*   *

Take that leap of faith. Take that small step and believe. Cryoterraform, Krys, you'll never forget it. It will haunt you. You'll always wonder what it would've looked like. Would Doctor Schwenne have been right? Would, would, would. All those questions unanswered. A hundred tiny suns, Krys. A form with spontaneity that grows and changes like a living thing before your very eyes. The next step, Krys, take it… Help us find the final absolute!"

I watched Krys grapple the demons in his mind. I heard the elevator approaching now.

00:29:00.

00:29:10.

Was he ever going to speak?

"Project IV is waiting for a call. There's two dozen security personnel on the surface waiting in case things don't go quietly."

00:29:20. 30.

Kendyll, bless her, didn't flinch, and in an instant I knew she too heard the elevator's approach. She continued her magnificently intent stare into the Krys's eyes. "Are you on the team?"

40.

A life's work. I saw the elevator now and glanced to the monitors.

50. 51. 52. 53.

Absolutes

Would it all be for nothing?

54. 55. 56.

The final absolute waited. The transition into the never before seen beyond, waited.

56. 57.

A hundred tiny suns. The point where matter isn't.

58.

I held my breath. My life swam before my eyes. The years of joy and toil with Kendyll at my side — would it all be worth it?

59.

The elevator stopped. Krys frowned. "It's too late. I can't stop them. They believe he's mad and that he's controlling you all."

Kendyll grabbed Krys's shoulders and shook him. "You are in control here, Krys. But are you on our team?"

Krys craned his neck to look at the trooper shouting to him to get out of the way. His eyes glazed over. I watched him grapple Beelzebub himself.

More troopers emerged from the elevator now, phase pistols drawn. I waited, my breath stuck in my lungs.

"Doctor Kendyll," Krys began, the glaze gone from his eyes, "How long does it take to run the array back up?"

Right then I was never so sure that I'd see those hundred tiny suns. The final absolute would be mine and Cryoterraform would change everything. I emerged from the shadows and

*   *

gave Kendyll a hug and then I turned to Krys. As I shook his hand, I said, "Welcome to the team, Dr. Steelbridge."

My eyes went wide with horror as Krys shook his head. "No, Dr. Schwenne. You don't understand. The array is going back online to take readings of the condensation state. Like I said, it's too late, they think you're mad. Even if I change my mind, they'll send another replacement — and another if that's what it takes."

I grabbed Krys by the shoulders and shook him. "No kid, you don't understand. I'm going to take it all with me." I waved my hands around the lab wildly. "Every last bit of it. Kiss it all goodbye!"

I started to shout an evacuation order as I ran toward the array controls. A moment later everything careened to blackness as I lost consciousness.

CHAPTER THREE: STRUGGLE AGAINST TIME

A trickle of blood ran down my cheek. I knew they'd kill me in the end, but I grinned at the monitor and began all the same. My thoughts were for Margaret's safety and not my own.

I took the four-hour shuttle from EOS-7 to Moon Colony to listen to an obscure scientist named Doctor Martin Schwenne, more specifically to hear his ideas on the future of space colonization, which he claimed was nonexistent. He also claimed progress in space travel was dead.

This astounded and attracted me. Especially since he was lecturing at Space Pro Labs which only a year ago had matched and then topped the previously thought

Absolutes

unattainable Earth-Moon Shuttle Speed Record of five hours set by Galactic Engineering a decade earlier. The five-hour record had lasted ten years. Space Pro Labs had broken it in grand style and in the process won total Earth-Moon Shuttle rights — a contract worth billions per day.

So where did this obscure scientist named Doctor Martin Schwenne get off proclaiming the era of progress in space colonization defunct?

For the most part, passage on the shuttle went smoothly. I gained entrance to the labs with a special clearance pass and was seated in the middle of the ninety-third row of the assembly hall exactly four hours twenty-eight minutes after departure from Earth Orbit Station Seven. A buzz of frenzy was sweeping through the crowd. I played my part, proudly relaying the latest gossip. But what everyone really wanted to know was: who was this Doctor Schwenne?

A tiny toothpick of a man wandered onto the stage. The crowd quieted. I think most thought, as did I, that the little man would introduce our speaker, Dr. Martin Schwenne, but as it turned out he was Dr. Martin Schwenne. I was shocked.

I settled back into my seat, vying for armrest space with my neighbors. On one side was a gaunt but thick-jawed man clad in prim business attire who undoubtedly hadn't slept in days. He was popping red beepers like they were candy. On the other sat the inevitable robust lecture-circuit attendee. He

*   *

slapped both corpulent forearms down onto the armrests with the intent of not moving either again until the meeting concluded. We conducted war with our elbows for a time.

Then without warning, Martin Schwenne's meek voice rang out. "Innerspace is a fraud. Cryodrives are a false hope!"

Needless to say, I jumped straight out of my seat and screamed back at him, "What do you mean innerspace is a fraud? What do you mean cryodrives are a false hope?"

Martin cleared his throat, his face pallid. I quickly settled into my seat and conducted armchair warfare with my neighbors again.

Martin Schwenne talked on. I jumped out of my seat two more times. I just couldn't help myself.

"Yank this man from the pulpit," I cried out when I just couldn't take it any more. The lectern at Space Pro Labs was sacred to me. It was here in 2391 that I had listened to Ishad Ballin defend his first dissertation after leaving Galactic Engineering in 2390.

I shrank back into my seat — only under the weight of several thousand pairs of withering eyes. Yet, I did notice that a handful of others had joined me to their feet.

I tuned back into the illustrious speaker, confident he would say nothing now that I would care to hear. Also sure that if I made a dash for the door those same withering stares would return. As I was tucked into the middle of the ninety-third row — a hard place to escape from easily — it would've been a long, solitary walk.

Martin was saying, "You've been fed spoonfuls of warped science about space since the inception of space colonization. In this modern day, there are still some who believe that the human body will explode if it hits the vacuum of space, yet you and I know this is hardly the case. Some will not travel on the shuttle because they're afraid of falling into the sun. Please, we know better."

Martin paused to rub his bifocals, the ancient spectacles, like him, a relic from the past. "I didn't choose these facts randomly. I chose them to show you past space colonization myths. But there are books still in print this very day by some of my colleagues who ought to know better than to go on and on about innerspace and cryoterraform. It is innerspace this and innerspace that, cryo this and cryo that. And then there are the technical journals that drone on and on about the meticulous and the monotonous, theorizing, always theorizing…"

I held my seat despite the urge to drag Doctor Schwenne from the pulpit.

"And they've effectively corrupted your receptiveness to new ideas, innovations and new technologies. There will never be a cryodrive or even a cryocoil… And as for innerspace, to steal an equally antiquated phrase, bah-humbug… It will never be reached!"

I jumped out of my seat again. I couldn't help myself. My face was red. I was short of breath. My heart was pounding in my ears. "Where did they find this clown? Didn't anyone screen him? Didn't anyone screen him?"

Others joined in and soon people started leaving, fanning out the doors. They'd never look back and while I was partly to blame, I felt no remorse. Dr. Schwenne stood there as calmly as you please and stared me down. I'm not sure if he could see all the way to the ninety-third row with his reading spectacles, but it sure seemed that way.

I surely saw him. A bright, white-yellow spotlight fixed on his bone-thin face and there was sweat beading on his ashened brow. His hands were trembling, but I didn't care.

"Anarchist! Anarchist!" I began to chant.

Several others joined in. "Anarchist, anarchist," we chanted.

Before I knew it, there were but three of us left in the whole of the auditorium, myself, someone in the far right wing, and the illustrious Dr. Martin Schwenne. The last of my anarchist chants drowned in my throat. But by this time, I felt too poorly to leave.

Dr. Schwenne cleared his throat one, two, three, four times. Then in his meek voice, he began again. As he spoke, I moved closer. After all, I had ruined his day. He may as well get a clear view of my face. The man in the far right wing didn't stir —

probably sleeping, or so I imagined.

I didn't tune back into Martin's speech until I was front row center.

"Heavenly objects," he was saying, "move in circular paths, you cannot fall into the sun. It is impossible. And yet, this is what people imagine every time the E-M shuttle trajectory goes errant. There is but one swift way to get from the Earth to the Moon and that is a linear path — two hundred and thirty-nine thousand miles in one great shot... In theory only of course, the trajectory isn't directly linear by any means..."

I yawned and momentarily fought off the urge to sleep, which would have been impolite.

"Time moves in linear paths, you can only journey forward in time, not back, never back. You can only look back. That was the thinking that the scientific community held for an epoch and thus when they measured space, distance, time and ultimately speed they similarly measured it in tangible means. First it was the speed of sound that was the ultimate barrier... 1100 feet-per-second at sea level. Whoopee! Can you imagine? Eleven hundred feet-per-second, children's toys are faster by today's standards. The next measurement chosen was the speed of light — one hundred and eighty-six thousand miles-per-second. Alas, a speed never to be attained for we were looking in the wrong direction."

Martin paused, wiped his eyes, continued. "Up until a

*   *

decade ago, the Earth-Moon Shuttle Speed Record held the highest recorded speed at an insignificant forty-eight thousand miles-per-hour. A year ago the sixty thousand miles-per-hour barrier was broken. New records will be achieved. However, innerspace and cryodrives will never be realized. In the beyond, all matter breaks down. Magnetohydrodynamic coils can only provide so much additional power."

"There simply is no way to break the barrier and achieve the unachievable. Am I correct, Doctor?" asked Dr. Schwenne pointing to a man in the audience.

The man in the far right wing nodded his head slightly, then Martin Schwenne continued. "Sound, measured in waves, vibrations transmitted through a medium. The human range of sound is limited, approximately twenty hertz to eight thousand hertz at optimum. Light, electromagnetic radiation, thought once to be corpuscular, then described as waves, and even as Quantum phenomenon. The wavelength visible to the naked eye 4,000 to 7,700 Angstrom units.

"Physical objects, described once quite innocently as the elements fire, water, air, and earth, comprised of molecules, atoms, and hundreds of smaller elements. Each new discovery a step closer to the infinitely minuscule. If we cannot see it, then it was never there — until we discover it. That's the thinking. That's what they said about quarks. Look what happened after that discovery.

Absolutes

"Oh sure, you can measure the ultrasonic. You can measure the ultraviolet and the infrared. Feynman would have been proud of the evolution of space-time diagrams. But if we cannot see it — measure it — then it was never there, even with quantum mechanics. For you see, conventional thinkers never change. Deep down they will always be conventional thinkers despite what they profess.

"We attached the same physical limitations to our way of realizing speed and breaching distance — space. We attached the phrases subsonic, supersonic, and hypersonic to measurements of speed. When that wasn't enough we raced to achieve light speed.

"We described space in the same manner, two dimensional, three dimensional, adding the element of time to obtain a forth dimension, finally settling on the hyperspatial as we raced to reach innerspace. We exploited space linearly and when that didn't fit the theory of innerspace we warped it, while still trying to remain within the bounds of our physical limitation laws. But we never achieved innerspace and we never achieved cryoterraform — those things beyond the braking off point, just at the brink of the thing we cannot attain. No one understand how the two are linked but—"

Front row center, I was sitting straight up in my chair, hands gripped to both armrests. Martin Schwenne's hands were trembling violently. His spectacles had slid down to the

*   *

very tip of his nose. I waited, breathless. What was the answer? What was the next stage in evolution for space colonization and for space travel? I wanted to know. I had to know. Surely there was more than four-hour shuttle rides to look forward to? Surely, we could reach innerspace and use the same forces to tap into cryoterra.

I waited and waited, with a lump that was my heart in my throat. Dr. Schwenne didn't say another word and he never did turn to look at me as he left the stage as I thought he would. I imagined that he had stopped there on the verge of revelation to torment me for what I had done. And it was then I realized that Martin Schwenne had probably given the best speech of his entire life and that there had been but two people to hear it.

CHAPTER FOUR: FADING MEMORIES

"Recorders off please," the voice said.

The hot white lights dimmed and I saw insolent eyes, a dark mop of hair, and eventually a thick-jawed face.

The man said, "What about the imagcam, you didn't mention it?"

"No," I said. "I never found the imagcam. The recordings are lost."

"So, why are you here then, Dr. Steelbridge?"

"Why?" I scratched my jaw and maintained the fight against their drugs. "I'm not quite sure. I could ask you why have you brought me here. What would you say if I did?"

Absolutes

*   *

"You were brought here for an evaluation and not by us. Yet I think the evaluation is complete, you are free to leave any time you wish."

"Free to leave?" I asked.

"Yes, free. Go any time you wish. Good-bye."

I got out of my chair; my legs seemed suddenly weak.

"Wait, where are you going?"

"You said I could leave, I'm going home."

"No, I said you were free to leave. Sit, please. I have one final question for you. Your memories of the event were quite complete, quite complete. Yet it seems you overlooked a few details. The story is too complete I am afraid, too complete."

"Which part do you want me to retract? I'll retract it."

"Do you recall the day EOS-7 Security brought you to us? Will you tell me about it?"

I offered a toothless grin, blood trickling down my cheek dropped into a pool forming on the tabletop. "Certainly…"

■ ■ ■

"Twenty-two minutes to shuttle departure," called out a mechanical-sounding feminine voice. I glanced at my wristwatch, headed for the pre-departure lounge.

A handful of eyes followed me in through the access way. I shrank into a corner and hurriedly gulped down the drink I had pre-ordered on the shuttle ride from Earth. Naturally, I tuned in to the conversation of the couple beside me.

Robert Stanek

*   *

"Oh, it was awful, dreadful, didn't you hear? He was to have been hired on at the end of the week—" The woman was sobbing and there were tears in her eyes. "—There was to be no more living off the doll, no more part-time for me, no more double overtime for him…"

"There, there, Margaret, things will work out right, they always do."

What a horrible thing to say, things don't always work out right.

"He can't go back to Galactic, not now. Five lectures and that was to be it, the contract would have been irrevocable… Ten years on Moon Colony would've been grand."

The woman's companion cooed. "Would've been grand indeed."

That's life, a roll of the dice. I listened, not so intently now. And the mechanical, feminine voice counted down the time.

Before I knew it, I was settling into one of those comfortable yet not-so-comfortable shuttle chairs — the ones with hardly any armrest space. Vying for my space was already a given. I plopped both arms down firmly before the fellow next to me could settle in.

Strapped in, I waited. I gleaned a pillow from a shuttle stewardess passing by. The hum of the overdrive engines during preflight checks caught my ear. I had never really thought about it before — sixty thousand miles-per-hour,

Absolutes

wow!

A disturbance cross-cabin caught my attention. A pencil-necked gentleman had spilled the contents of his vacuum case. Books and papers were everywhere. And there was Margaret — poor faithful Margaret — at the man's side. She was scooping papers from the floor and putting them back into the vacuum case. The man just stood there, his face buried in his hands.

I did my part, picking up the scattered papers near my seat. Margaret sobbed through several heartfelt thanks. The man never looked over to me, not even once and I must've put four or five stacks of assorted papers and books back into that vacuum bag.

Afterward, Margaret took the man's hand and led him away. It was a sad sight. I heard her female companion's voice cooing to her a moment later, "There, there Margaret, don't cry."

I grabbed a blanket from a passing stewardess, closed my eyes even though I'd never been able to sleep on the E-M shuttle.

Three hours fifty-nine minutes later, the shuttle was approaching Earth Orbit Station-7 for docking. The familiar mechanical service voice called out, "E. O. S. Seven. Docking procedures underway."

My seat rocked as retros kicked in. Four and a half minutes

*   *

later, I was eagerly stepping from my seat. Had to beat the crowd, only six minutes till the next shuttle to the surface. If I missed it, it would mean a fifteen-minute wait I couldn't afford — fifteen minutes subtracted from the two hours I had scheduled for sleep. I had a full day after those two hours sleep — another twenty-four-hour day and red beepers only nurtured so long.

Midstride I noticed it. It looked innocent enough, a single piece of paper strewn next to my chair. Several others beside it were partially obscured by the chair. I picked up the papers, but I didn't look at them as I had first thought to. They had to belong to Margaret's man.

I folded them in half, stuffed them into my pocket. I turned back to grab my briefcase, and by that time, the insidious crowd had already formed in front of me. There was no way I'd make the first shuttle now. I'd have to wait the fifteen minutes.

■■■

The hot white light was turned off again. The mop of dark hair slowly fell before my eyes.

The voice said, "How long have you been here?"

"Two weeks."

"Two weeks?" The man sighed. "Two years."

I agreed. "Yes, two years."

"Two years, are you sure?"

I shrugged.

Absolutes

"See, you're not sure anymore, are you? Take me back to EOS-7. Tell me about the imagcam."

The hot white light returned.

CHAPTER FIVE: FINAL SALUTE

The fifteen-minute wait had been ugly and quite ungodly. But there I was strapped in again, last seat on the left of the five hundred twenty-second row waiting to enter Earth's atmosphere.

EOS-7 had been crowded. Too crowded. And there had been endless lines everywhere.

I felt the first ripples and braced for reentry. Descending into Earth's atmosphere was akin to riding a stellar wave until it slammed into the face of the moon. Quick, short, bumpy, and sometimes deadly.

A few seconds passed. Things started to smooth out. I

cursed myself for paying ten thousand credits for the hundred-million-credit aborted-entry insurance. Then without warning, the shuttle lurched to a halt.

Naturally, I filed out of the shuttle and eventually filtered into the line with everyone else waiting for the three-minute fifteen-second shuttle to New L.A. In the crowd were Margaret, her female companion and the pencil-necked man with the vacuum bag. Margaret's lady friend was still cooing in her ear.

"There, there Margaret," she was still saying.

Margaret was sobbing and blowing her nose into a saturated handkerchief.

Recalling the papers in my pocket, the spilled vacuum bag and how I felt about poor Margaret, I made a dash for her. But she was soon lost in the insidious crowd.

I continued the search for a moment — only a moment. I had but one minute to be strapped in on the three-minute fifteen-second shuttle to New L.A. I didn't find her, so I turned and dashed back to the departure bay. The hold line had shifted and I had to conduct a limited assault campaign to get my place back.

A siren sounded. A lull swept through the crowd. The mechanical service voice called out, "The three-minute fifteen-second shuttle to New L.A. has been delayed by two minutes forty-five seconds."

A murmur erupted from the crowd. I shrank against the

*   *

wall, held onto my briefcase with a death grip. In an instant, this would get ugly. The last time this had happened they had to cordon off three departure bays and airport security in full riot gear had to be called in.

"I have deadlines to meet!" shouted one man.

Another screamed, "I want my money back!"

Several others carried on his chant.

Far behind me and to the right, I heard a woman crying. I had nothing to lose now. I peered through the stirring mob. It was Margaret, poor, sad Margaret. The announcement must've been too much for her. I could see her female companion cooing into her ear. The man with his vacuum bag sat still, slumped over onto his haunches with his face buried in his hands. Poor, sad Margaret.

I recalled the papers in my pocket. Surely the papers would cheer her up. Ninety-eight seconds remained in the delay, so I made a heroic dash.

The crowd growing irate, didn't bend. I had to fight my way through, wielding my briefcase before me. I had played full contact hyberball more than a few times, but things here were different. These guys really wanted to hurt me. I managed, barely, to weave my way through to Margaret.

I unfolded the small stack of papers nicely, taking out the creases the way a gentleman would. I handed the papers to Margaret, only then glancing at the imprinted words. The first

*   *

page of a technical manuscript stared back at me. It was entitled:

Space Colonization is Dead

And underneath the manuscript header and title were these words:

Written by

Dr. Martin Schwenne
&
Dr. Ishad Ballin

I paused briefly to look at the gentleman whose face was still buried in his hands. I wanted to say something, though I didn't know what. Poor, sad Margaret, someone had to brighten her day.

"Things will turn out all right, they always do," I said, smiling though I didn't believe it.

Margaret's sobs intensified. I turned away. The delay was over. The angry mob became a crowd. I was nearly late for the three-minute fifteen-second shuttle to New L.A. Halfway to the shuttle doors, I realized something. It struck me like a ball of red lightning and my legs froze. Dr. Ishad Ballin had been in

*   *

the Space Pro Labs auditorium — the one person I idolized was working with Dr. Martin Schwenne. Then I realized something else.

I looked back over my shoulder, but Margaret, her female companion and the illustrious Martin Schwenne, were gone. I stood there for what seemed the longest time. Minutes may have passed; I'm not quite sure. Then I hurried off.

I missed the three-minute fifteen-second shuttle to New L.A. — not because I couldn't have made it. The stewardess had already taken my boarding pass. The countdown timer had been ticking away. The departure bay doors were closing as I looked on. I was one step away, but I didn't move. I didn't want to move. I didn't want to hurry off. I had done what I had set out to do, what I had been hired to do, for you see, that is what I do.

My hands trembling just as violently as Martin Schwenne's hands had been trembling hours earlier, I unclasped my briefcase. I emptied its contents, including the imagcam, into the nearest refuse receptacle. No immediate second thoughts, I strode off.

Then I got to thinking. I never should have accepted payment from Galactic Project IV on such an issue yet could I let forty million credits slip away? The answer was right there before me. No, I couldn't.

I hurried back to the receptacle.

Absolutes

I reached my hand into the trash and groped around. But it wasn't there. I screamed, "Dear God, it's gone, it's gone," then proceeded to tear the receptacle off the wall. Trash sprayed into the corridor. On hands and knees, I groped my way through it. But there was no imagcam. And forty million credits slipped away in an instant because I was going soft. Soft, could you imagine? Me, soft.

I searched through that trash until EOS-7 Security carried me away. I never found the imagcam. I never received the final installment.

■■■

"Mr. Steelbridge, you've told that story the same way every time, except this last time. What did you change this last time? What is it that you no longer wish to tell us?" The man sucked in a breath ominously. "What if I told you we recovered something of yours from the EOS-7 disposers, what then? I'll ask one last time, what happened to the imagcam?"

I offered an ugly smile. "I gave it to Margaret."

"And Dr. Schwenne?"

"No."

"What do you mean by that? And I'll thank you to wipe that smile off your face." The man waited for my expression to change, but it didn't. Then he repeated, "What do you mean by that?"

"I mean, no. No is what I mean."

*   *

The man's spidery arm reached out for my shirt and wrenched me across the table.

I maintained my grin. They would kill me, but I had already won. Margaret was safe by now and Martin's dangerous thoughts were lost in corners of my mind that could never be freed. Then I said the words I had been waiting to say. "The future of space colonization is hardly dead, my dear man. It is dawning…"

The man bunched his eyebrows together.

"And you see, nothing you do to me matters. I've paid my debt. And even if you did recover the imagcam, I erased the parts worth your while and destroyed every digital record of Martin's ideas that ever existed outside of his mind."

I pried the man's hand from my shirt and shuttled across the table to my seat. The man followed, a syringe in his hand.

Momentarily, I paraded my dignity while I waited for the end. Then I said proudly the last words I'd ever speak. "You see, Martin really did perfect cryoterraform and the cryodrive… It is only a matter of time now."

As the world faded to black, I heard Martin say in the back of my mind, "Instead of looking to go faster, we should have been looking to go slower, the final absolute, where matter is at once infinitely still and infinitely fast. The final absolute where matter becomes something new — something that will change space and become at once, the key and the coffer."

Bonus Excerpt From:
In the Service of Dragons

Amir, son of Ky'el, cast the orb at his feet and stepped into a spinning circle of light. "They've arrived in the high desert; the field is set. The others will come now. I only pray that all will not be lost."

"You lose faith," the other replied without looking up. "You must be patient. In the end, the paths will come together. It is so written."

"Can nothing change the course we have set upon?"

"You could no sooner catch the moon or the wind. Once set in motion, it will not stop. For now we must wait and watch. Our time will come soon enough."

Absolutes

"Would you have me follow them?"

"Go to the clansman, Ashwar Tae. Tell him it is time."

Amir stepped back into the spinning circle of light, disappearing and reappearing on the windswept slopes of the Rift. He appeared alongside a man on horseback and asked, "Big enough for you?" The man had the disciplined look of a soldier. He had a wide mouth, a long, sharp nose and a head of wildly unkempt copper-colored curls. He was dressed in boiled leather padded with a thick fur lining and studded with many rows of sharp steel teeth. A great sword was slung on his back and a quartet of throwing knives hung from his studded leather belt.

The man turned to grin at Amir, his few good teeth showing amongst the bad. "Indeed. It is just as you said," he declared, reaching out to grip the other's forearm. "You have kept your word, and I thank you for that."

"Don't thank me, Ashwar, thank him."

Ashwar turned back to the procession of giants, beasts, and men, thinking to himself that he'd sooner thank the Fourth himself than the King of Titans. The one was the devil he knew, the other the devil in his life—or so it seemed to him.

For hours, the two watched the procession without speaking further. The giants of the six clans lumbered by—fire and ice, storm and mountain, stone and hill. The beastmen of the Lost Lands, atop mammoths, rode by six abreast, trumpets

*   *

roaring. Behind them came the Dragon Men of the Ice. Some of the Dragon Men rode great bears—black, white or brown. Others rode great wolves, either gray or white. His clansmen, the men, women and children of Oshywon, came last. Some were afoot but most were ahorse like him.

In the stories of old, Ashwar had heard of Gatherings, but he never imagined he would see one in his lifetime, let alone help to assemble it. He was excited and frightened at the same time. In the stories, Gatherings marked the end of an age and always finished badly. He wondered how this time could be any different, but he had hope. Hope was all his people clung to at times—hope for a better tomorrow, a better life, hope for a return to the plains and rivers they once knew, hope for justice and retribution, hope for their children or their children's children if not for themselves.

"Has it happened then?" he finally asked Amir.

Amir turned and knelt beside the man on horseback, staring at him eye to eye. "It has."

Ashwar cinched his horse's bridle in his hand and held him still. In the stories of old, Titans had ruled over men and elves, and Amir had the qualities of a ruler. Even with him ahorse and Amir kneeling, the Titan towered over him and it was hard to say how big he really was. Twelve feet tall maybe or fourteen, Ashwar thought, maybe taller. His broad chest and muscular arms made him seem bigger, much bigger, like some sort of towering oak that had been uprooted and transformed. But his face wasn't brutish and square like a giant's. It was refined and round, very manlike, just unusually proportioned, with a jutting chin, high cheekbones, and dark eyes so large and deep-set that they seemed high mountain caverns, or perhaps wells, whose depths swept to the Titan's very soul.

One of the giants guarding the van of the procession came upon them. He was larger than most of the others and the fire showed clearly in his features: the long auburn-colored hair and beard, the eerie red of his eyes. He was wearing the pelt of several great bears roughly sown together and was carrying a thick spear that looked like an uprooted evergreen trimmed and sharpened yet otherwise whole. He spoke to Amir in Giantspeak and the Titan responded in kind.

"It is a good day, he says, as good a day as any," Amir told Ashwar when the giant departed.

Ashwar looked about uneasily. "A good day for what?"

"Exactly what I asked him before he hurried off to rejoin the van. Giants may be lumbering and big, but they can be hasty as well."

"Lumbering and big is an understatement."

Amir laughed as he stood—the laughter like the deep rumbling of distant thunder. "I must return. You know what must be done now?"

"I do, and I thank you for coming."

*   *

"Goodbye then, until we meet again," and so saying, Amir cast the orb at his feet and stepped into the spinning circle of light.

As he emerged from shadow, Amir found Noman playing at Destiny Sticks. He went to a window without saying a word but it was not the view beyond that he was interested in—it was Noman. Seated with a hunch-backed posture, Noman seemed a small man; yet standing with his shoulders back and straight, he seemed regal. Amir didn't know whether it was the veins of black that streaked otherwise pure white hair, the eyebrows with matching spikes of black mixed with gray or the beard that flowed to the middle of his chest in a sheet of pure silver that made Noman seem a king, but he seemed a king nonetheless—and a great king at that. But Noman was not a king; he was but a man who lived among Titans in the City of the Sky.

"It seems so futile, this waiting," Amir complained.

Noman cast the sticks upon the table, looking up momentarily to regard the other. In girth, Amir's shoulders spread from one side of the grand window to the other, filling its opening when he turned his back to the light. "And when the wait is over, what then?"

Amir didn't answer. Instead he watched as Noman played at the game of Destiny, carefully picking out the black and white sticks representing the Path, avoiding the gray sticks of the Void. Lost in the rhythm of the game, his thoughts soon carried him into the distant past.

"Are we then outside time?" a much younger Amir asked the figure in his mind's eye.

"Time affects all things, even those who consider themselves outside its grasp."

"But why me? Why me when there were so many others more deserving?"

"It is as it must be."

"But I have done nothing to receive so great an honor."

"That is untrue. You were the most skilled of your kind ever to walk the earth."

"You talk in the past; am I not dead then?"

Noman smiled. "Back to the same question. Your thoughts move in circles. You know you are not. The Father has true need of your skills when the time is right."

While in the waking world Noman's hands busily worked the sticks, Amir's thoughts slipped further into the past. To his right, Antwar Alder, the man who would be king, swept Truth Bringer from its sheath, the great blade seeming to outshine the moon with its own inner light and lending a pale shadow over the strong-faced Antwar.

Ky'el touched his arm. "Ready yourself, son."

An adolescent Amir nodded. "I swore an oath, a holy oath I mean to keep."

*   *

"There are more," whispered Etry. "Where are Aven and Riven?"

Amir looked down the line. The city's outer defenses had failed and the last of the defenders made their stand at the Greye, the very keep built by their enemy Dnyarr. Across Gregortonn's High Square the first charge of the night began with the cracks of whips from the goblin lieutenants sending the dog packs into a frenzied, howling run. The lines of human slaves followed; and behind them came the chariots of the elves pulled by the black, wingless dragons of the Samguinne.

Ky'el thundered toward the line, his silver cloak streaming from his shoulders. Amir tried to follow.

Dust seemed to be blowing everywhere. Keeping up with the shadowy figure charging into the battle required his full attention.

The besiegers began screaming and cheering as the packs set into the lines, their screams and cheers in stark contrast to the cries of pain from the defenders, the sound of it all very nearly blocking out the strange whistling from above. By the time Amir saw the first black-feathered arrow strike one of his fellows, it was too late.

An arrow hit him full in the chest, piercing his breastplate. An instant later, he found himself on the other side. "Am I dead or am I dreaming?" he asked himself as he floated in the void.

"Not dead," said the voice from out of the void—the voice

Absolutes

Amir would in later years come to know as Noman's. "Your path continues far beyond this place."

"Where am I? Why am I here?"

"Ky'el's time comes to an end. *Look*, the arrow has pierced his heart, not yours." It was the first use of the compelling voice Amir had encountered and it was in that moment that he realized he was cradling Ky'el—that the arrow had pierced Ky'el's armor not his own.

Hot tears streamed down his cheeks. The battle was all but over.

"What am I to do?"

"You shall find out soon. Now is not the time."

"What is this place?"

"The world of dreams and reality are closely knit, very closely knit," Noman said. "Ofttimes the two appear as one and the same, or perhaps another. Some exist in a state of perpetual dream, others in a state of eternal life, and a few in a state of the dream within their eternal life. You, my young friend, find the dream at a time when life's need is at its greatest."

Amir was halfway through a response when he realized he was back in the present, sitting in the great window with the fading sun casting his shadow long upon the floor. Hours had passed. Noman had laid out the final path upon the table. "Is it—?" he started to ask but was interrupted.

*   *

"Must you always dwell in the past?" Noman asked.

"There, you see, even when I think, I cannot be alone."

"That is as it must be. Come, even you must eat. Ah, and before you complain, this is what you wanted. I know it is."

Amir looked at the food spread out in front of him like a feast. "Yes, but I changed my mind."

"No you didn't. You shouldn't fool with an old man's mind."

"An old man? You are the one who taught me that appearance is meaningless."

Noman's eyes flashed. "Appearance is everything; you would do well to remember that."

Amir made no further comment and instead ate until he was content then walked back to his window to continue his watch. Time passed without change. As Noman stared at the Destiny Sticks and busily consulted his books, Amir waited in silence as the sun disappeared over the horizon.

The next day brought more restlessness. Amir paced back and forth, occasionally glancing out the window. Both he and Noman could sense a change, a presence that could not be explained in words. Noman didn't show his anxiety as much as Amir did although within he was indeed anxious. He could sense it just as much as Amir could.

Seeking to ease the tension, Noman began to concentrate, focusing his thoughts, cycling the Magicks through his body discreetly. His hope was to catch Amir off guard; but after centuries of being with Noman, Amir responded to the attack with catlike grace, unsheathing his goliath, double-edged bastard sword, turning, lifting, and striking out at his invisible opponent in the time it took most to inhale a single breath.

The resonant clang of metal striking metal soon filled the air. Amir knew his opposition well; after all, it was himself. He fought his own shadow as always and it knew his every move, his every trick. It remembered each time that Amir had overcome it in the past. It fed on those defeats so that each time Amir was forced to think differently or to act differently, thus improving his performance or making him stronger and faster so he could defeat it.

He charged repeatedly, wielding his weapon with the ease and skill of a master, the generous weight of its mass carefully balanced in his hands. He attempted a simple combination, thrust, parry, thrust, followed quickly by a thrust, slice, and a feint. The shadow seemed to mock him as it followed his every move and counter.

"Will I ever be able to fight this beast in reality?" Amir asked, gritting his teeth, circling left.

"Concentrate," Noman responded, "Concentrate or you will become the shadow."

Amir dropped, rolled and thrust upward with his blade. The shadow blocked and circled.

"It seems so fruitless, all this training, all this waiting. What

*   *

will happen then, afterward?"

Noman raised his eyebrows, sensing the intent in the words. "Do not fret so. The day comes, revel in that, but trust me when I say you will wish it hadn't."

Through the afternoon the assault continued. Amir's blade broke the air about him wildly, pushing the shadow into a corner. He was nearly winded but he couldn't let his fatigue show. The shadow had an advantage over him. It never tired, it was relentless, it learned with every breath. So even as Amir moved in for the kill, the shadow countered and waited for the lunge that was meant to end its existence; then it cackled in delight.

As Amir's blade met empty air, he shouted, "This is going nowhere!"

"Your mind is overly occupied elsewhere. You should not be thinking of Ashwar and the clansmen! Focus upon what is important!"

"Concentrate, concentrate," Amir exhorted himself. Nearing exhaustion, his only resource left was a gambit. He jumped into the air. Midway through a forward somersault, he struck down, only to slice empty air.

He landed, recovered from the momentary surprise, dodged a well-timed blow from the shadow, spun, and then hurled his sword outward. This time his blade struck true and the creature roared its defeat. The shadow had done exactly what Amir expected it to do. It had dodged his first attack and tried to attack him from behind as he landed. The next sweep of the creature's blade should have caught him except that Amir spun to the right instead of to the left where the shadow had been; and as it countered, Amir struck outward with the lethal blow, ending the match in victory as always.

Sweat glistening from his muscular body, Amir sheathed his sword and wiped perspiration from his brow. He was tired, very tired, though he would not show it. He had learned from the shadow as much as it had learned from him and he would not forget the lesson. Steadying himself, he returned to the great window and his vigil.

That evening the two supped in silence, lost in thought. As the last light of the day gave way to the darkness of the night, Noman looked up from his books. "You must be patient. Watch, but take no action." His guarded expression said everything. The hour had come; the long wait was over. Amir cast the orb at his feet, but before he could step into the spinning circle of light, Noman spoke again. "Heed my warning, take no action. Watch, and when it is over, return to report."

Amir stepped into the circle of light, disappearing and reappearing on the desolate sands of the Barrens. The air in the high mountain desert was chill and growing colder by the moment as the wind sucked the warmth of the day from the

*   *

sand. In the distance he could see a bonfire, its dull orange glow a beacon in the darkness. Two figures moved around the fire; but it was the third, lying in sleep, that interested him the most. He called out a challenge to the wind and waited.

About the Author: The Short (Not-So-Boring) Bio

Absolutes, *Silence is Golden*, and *August Rains* are among the earliest stories Robert Stanek wrote. Robert is an award-winning, international best-selling author of more than 65 books for young people and adults. He lives with his wife and children in the Pacific Northwest in the United States, and is intensely fascinated with our natural world. He loves the outdoors and frequently takes his family on short trips to see the natural wonders of the Pacific Northwest, including Mount Rainier, Mount St. Helens, the Columbia River Gorge, and Puget Sound.

About the Author: The Long (Possibly Kind of Boring) Bio

 Robert Stanek has written numerous best-selling, award-winning books for young people and adults. Robert was born in Burlington Wisconsin. He is the second youngest of five children. In 1985 he enlisted in the Air Force and entered a 2-year training program in Intelligence and Linguistics at the Defense Language Institute. After graduation he served in various field operations duties in Asia and Europe. In 1990 he won an appointment to Air Combat School and shortly after graduation served in the Persian Gulf War as a combat crewmember on an electronic warfare aircraft. During his two tours in the Persian Gulf War, Robert flew numerous combat and combat support missions, logging over two hundred combat flight hours. His distinguished accomplishments during the war earned him nine medals, including the United States of America's highest flying honor, the Air Force Distinguished Flying Cross, the Air Medal, the Air Force Commendation Medal, and the Humanitarian Service Medal. He earned 29 decorations in his 11-year military career.

Born into a family of readers, Robert was always reading and creating stories. Even before he started school, he read classics like Treasure Island, The Swiss Family Robinson, Kidnapped, Robinson Crusoe, and The Three Musketeers. Later in his childhood, he started reading Jules Verne, Sir Arthur Conan Doyle, Edgar Rice Burroughs, Ray Bradbury, Herman Melville, Jack London, Charles Dickens, and Edgar Allan Poe. Of that he says,

"Edgar Allan Poe can be pretty bleak and dark, especially when you're ten years old. But I remember being fascinated with his stories."

Robert completed his first novel in 1986 when he was stationed in Japan but it wasn't until nearly a decade later that his first book was published. After writing his master's thesis on the Internet and electronic publishing revolution, his professor encouraged him to get it published and that is exactly what he set out to do. His first book became a bestseller as did his next two books. Since then, he has written and had published more than 65 books.

Robert has won many awards from his colleagues and the publishing industry. Currently, he resides in the Pacific Northwest with his wife and children. For fun he used to spend a lot of time mountain biking and hiking, but now his adventures in the great outdoors are mostly restricted to short treks around the Pacific Northwest.

Learn more at
www.robertstanek.com

Enter the world of Ruin Mist
www.ruinmistmovie.com

The Kingdoms and the Elves of the Reaches

Don't miss this bestselling series…

In the Service of Dragons – The sequel series to
The Kingdoms and the Elves of the Reaches

Discover what happens when the dragons are revealed…

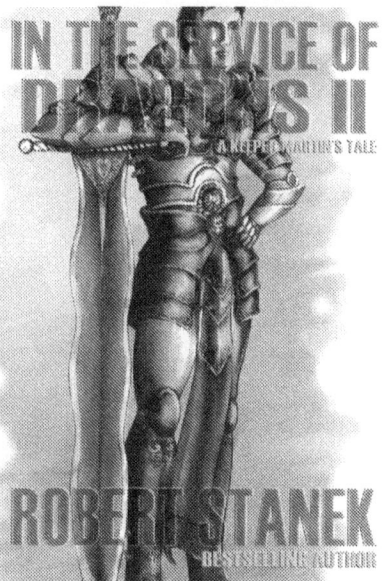

www.ingramcontent.com/pod-product-compliance
Lightning Source LLC
Chambersburg PA
CBHW020533120726
47904CB00003B/1061